DEC   2011

HARRY CONNICK, JR.

The Happy Elf

Illustrated by
Dan Andreasen

HARPER

An Imprint of HarperCollinsPublishers

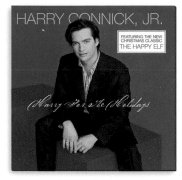

Available at: http://www.sonymusicdigital.com/harry-connick-jr/details/5089277

The Happy Elf Book and CD
Text and illustrations copyright © 2011 by HC Productions, Inc. and Film Roman LLC
Story based on the song "The Happy Elf" from *Harry for the Holidays* by Harry Connick, Jr.

Library of Congress Cataloging-in-Publication Data

Connick, Harry.
    The happy elf / written by Harry Connick, Jr. ; illustrated by Dan Andreasen. — 1st ed.
       p.   cm.
    Summary: An irrepressibly happy elf defies Santa's rules in order to make sure the residents of Bluesville are not sad at Christmastime.
    ISBN 978-0-06-128879-1
    [1. Elves—Fiction.   2. Christmas—Fiction.]   I. Andreasen, Dan, ill.   II. Title.
PZ7.C7628Hap   2010   2009029705
[E]—dc22   CIP
                                                                       AC

Typography by Jennifer Rozbruch
11 12 13 14 15 SCP 10 9 8 7 6 5 4 3 2 1

❖

First Edition

this book is dedicated to my mother, anita.
and sacks of love for j, g, k, and c!!!
—H.C.

for katrina
—D.A.

Eubie was the happiest elf at the North Pole. He loved working in Santa's magical workshop. He loved making toys for good girls and boys. He loved playing with his friends Gilda and Derek.

Most of all, Eubie LOVED Christmas.

At Christmastime he would wake up early each morning and yell, "YIPPPPPPPPEEEEEEEE!" as loud as his little elf vocal cords would let him.

Eubie's dream was to join Santa on his sleigh, delivering toys. Every year, Eubie hoped to make the sleigh team. Every year, Eubie was disappointed.

But even then he was still the happiest elf around. In fact, other elves thought he was a little TOO happy.

His whistling distracted them.

His dancing knocked over toys.

His early-morning "YIPPPPPPPEEEEEEEE!"s woke the reindeer.

Something had to be done!

One Christmas Eve morning, the head elf gave Eubie a job where he couldn't get in anyone's way: checking the naughty and nice lists.

Eubie checked the lists . . . and checked them twice.

Then he discovered something odd. Something unheard of! In the whole town of Bluesville, there was not one child on the nice list!

Eubie checked the lists a THIRD time.

But there was no mistake—EVERY child in Bluesville had been naughty. Which meant NOBODY would get presents!

If only Bluesville could get on the nice list before Christmas. But how could a whole town of naughty children become nice in just one day?

Good-hearted Eubie thought about how to help. He thought some more. And finally . . .

"I know!" he exclaimed. "I'll use my magic
hat to go to Bluesville and spread Christmas
cheer!" He ran to tell his friends.

"But Eubie," Gilda worried, "you'll break
Santa's most important rule—NEVER use
your magic hat outside the North Pole."

"You'll never make the sleigh team if
Santa finds out," Derek sighed.

"Those kids deserve a happy Christmas,
and I'm going to help!" Eubie said.

He pulled his magic hat down over his
eyes . . . then his chin . . . then all the way to his toes and . . .

WHOOSH!

He was gone.

POP! Eubie stood in the middle of an empty, dark street in the middle of an empty, dark town at the bottom of a valley so deep it seemed sunlight could never reach it.

No wonder everyone is on the naughty list, Eubie thought. *Bluesville feels like the saddest place in the world.*

Eubie saw some kids throwing rocks at one another.

"Whoa!" Eubie yelled. "Don't you know it's not nice to throw rocks?"

"We're playing catch. And they're not rocks, they're unburnable coal," one girl said.

"Unburnable WHAT?" Eubie asked.

"Unburnable coal. It's what these mountains are made of. Since it doesn't burn, the only thing it's good for is throwing!" She tossed a chunk to Eubie. "I'm Molly. Who are you, anyway?"

Eubie stuck the coal in his pocket. "I'm Eubie, and I'm here to show Bluesville the true spirit of Christmas!"

"Christmas? Who needs Christmas?" Molly sparked.
"GET LOST!"

This was going to be harder than Eubie thought. He
needed a plan! Eubie pulled his magic hat down to his toes
and . . . ***WHOOSH!***

He was gone.

POP!

As soon as Eubie got back to the North Pole, he was sent to Santa's office. "Am I in trouble?" Eubie asked.

"Eubie, Eubie, Eubie." Santa frowned. "You know the first rule my elves learn is to use their magic hats *only* around the North Pole. I'm afraid I have to take your hat."

Eubie told Gilda and Derek what had happened.

"You gave up your hat *and* the sleigh team to help those children," Gilda said. "Eubie, you have to try again. Here, take *my* hat!"

Eubie gasped.

"Thanks, Gilda! But I still need a plan. . . ."

Derek scratched his head.

Gilda paced.

Eubie stuck his hands in his pockets sadly. Suddenly . . .

"Unburnable coal!" he exclaimed.

"Unburnable WHAT?" Derek asked.

"Unburnable coal!" Eubie pulled the coal from his pocket.
It looked different. Where it had rubbed against the cloth, it
now shone as brightly as the sun.

Eubie's eyes lit up. "I've got it! First, I need just two things. . . ."

He pulled Gilda's hat over his eyes . . . then his chin . . .
then all the way to his toes and . . . ***WHOOSH!***

He was gone.

POP!

"Hi, Molly."

Molly jumped. "YOU again?"

"I told you—I'm here to spread Christmas cheer!" Eubie said. He had a jar of super-duper unburnable coal polish and a Christmas tree!

"What if unburnable coal is good for something besides throwing—something that would make Bluesville a brighter, happier place?" Eubie asked. "Would you help me?"

"Why not?" Molly said. "There's nothing else to do."

"Let's get to work!" shouted Eubie.

Eubie, Molly, and her friends polished the mountains of coal that rose from their dark valley floor all the way to the sky. Soon the sun was reflecting off the polished coal, lighting up the town below.

"Nothing like a little teamwork and goodwill to make a city shine!" said Eubie.

But they weren't done yet.

It was time to put up the tree.

Eubie and the children hung ornaments and strung garlands. And as Molly placed the star on top, the townsfolk gathered around.

"What in the world is this?" an old woman asked.

"This is a little something I like to call a Christmas tree," Eubie said. "Bluesville may be at the bottom of a dark valley, but it doesn't have to be a sad place. Ready, Molly?"

"Ready!" Molly turned on the tree lights.

As they twinkled, the lights reflected off the gleaming coal mountains until the entire town glimmered like a treasure chest of shining jewels.

"We got tired of having coal fights . . . so now we have coal *lights*!" Molly grinned.

Soon everyone else in Bluesville was smiling, too. Hands were held, songs were sung, and the spirit of Christmas glowed as brightly as the glorious tree in the town square.

"Congratulations, Molly. And congratulations, Bluesville!" Eubie proclaimed. "Now you know that love, togetherness, and goodwill are the secret to a happy Christmas—and to a happy *every* day!"

Eubie pulled Gilda's hat over his eyes, then his chin, then all the way to his toes, and . . .

WHOOSH!

He was gone.

POP!

Back at the North Pole, Santa was waiting for Eubie.

"Am I in trouble?" Eubie asked.

"Eubie, Eubie, Eubie," Santa said. "There is one rule at my workshop that is even *more* important than the most important rule."

"What's that?" Eubie asked.

"To put others first," Santa explained. "You have shown true kindness to others, and I'd like you to be part of my sleigh team tonight." Santa smiled. "And for showing kindness to *Eubie*, I would like to invite Gilda and Derek to join us on the sleigh as well. First stop, Bluesville!"

"YIPPPPPPPEEEEEEEEEE!" cried Derek.

"YIPPPPPPPEEEEEEEEEE!" squealed Gilda.

"YIIIIIIIIIPPPPPPPPPPPPEEEEEEEEEEEEEEEEE!" yelled Eubie.

Then Santa and the THREE happiest elves at the North Pole got into the sleigh. And with a wave and a shout of "Merry Christmas!" and a . . .

They were gone.